SO TIME
STOOD STILL

SO TIME
STOOD STILL

RENATO BETTIO

Halo Publishing International
7550 W IH-10 #800, PMB 2069,
San Antonio, TX 78229

First Edition, March 2025
ISBN: 978-1-63765-742-3
Library of Congress Control Number: 2024927327

Halo Publishing International is a self-publishing company that publishes adult fiction and non-fiction, children's literature, self-help, spiritual, and faith-based books. We continually strive to help authors reach their publishing goals and provide many different services that help them do so. We do not publish books that are deemed to be politically, religiously, or socially disrespectful, or books that are sexually provocative, including erotica. Halo reserves the right to refuse publication of any manuscript if it is deemed not to be in line with our principles. Do you have a book idea you would like us to consider publishing? Please visit www.halopublishing.com for more information.

So the reader says,

"I would love to read the most beautiful book on earth."

So the author humbly answers, "I would like this book to give you the epitome of what you hope for."

With gratitude

Table of Contents

Chapter I

A Day Like
Any Other

After the accident, things began to change between Rosa Irene and Pablo Armando. But it wasn't obvious until the moment they both decided to face each other and mend the disagreements before continuing on. This change was about the direction they had to go next, and that had been agreed upon years before the accident, though the event itself had forced them to discuss those little setbacks that, really, didn't require a solution.

One July afternoon, circumstances pointed them to the beginning of the journey. Memory traced the specific routes to follow, and they remembered those old catalogs that describe the attractions of one country or another, one city or another. They went over the places they wanted to visit and realized, before taking that first step that would last forever, the catalog had a note on one of its corners: "Leave now the here, the maybe, and the possible."

It was no longer necessary to discuss the date, time, or second they must get on the road; they already understood, as they traced their path, that between them there existed only the certainty that they had chosen the correct option. And so they would follow this road until no longer necessary, until fate dictated a drastic change of course.

They shared an indelible bond: a fondness for the arts. That's what initially brought them together; they first met in an abstract-art exhibit, at the Palacio de Bellas Artes, held by one of the city's galleries. They met again at a piano concert by the national symphony orchestra, which was sponsored by a convent on the outskirts of the city. A friendship was born; then it became a romantic relationship that eventually intertwined their lives.

They were of one mind, their thoughts mirroring one another. When considering the next step on their path, the answer was an immediate echo of "The Louvre in Paris!"

With the unsureness of those who want to predict the intention of the artist in their work, they had always wondered at the reason behind the enigmatic smile of *La Gioconda*. Did she have a secret or know a sacred detail about the genius who painted her?

Hand in hand, they wandered the ancient corridors of the Louvre, starting with the antiquities in the basement. They looked at each other as they reread the chisels in the black rock that dictate the rules in the Code of Hammurabi. Inexplicably, they understood the ancient Babylonian language in which the laws were written. This filled them with surprise and satisfaction. Likewise, using the Rosetta Stone, they understood the meaning of the Egyptian hieroglyphics on the walls of the tombs and the sarcophagi of the pharaohs.

They rushed up the stairs to the level that houses some of the most valuable paintings in the world, and in an instant, they stood before the display case that protected the legendary *Gioconda*. Staring into her eyes, they found the reflection of an irrational and incomprehensible image: the painter was naked. Again, they looked at each other and nodded, agreeing that that secret would never be revealed to any creature below their level of consciousness.

As they hastily exited the enormous museum, they decided to visit the Avenue des Poètes in the sixth *arrondissement* (the sixth neighborhood) of Paris. They entered a small café and sat in a corner, on two little chairs at an even smaller table. Memories filled their minds as they relived their wonderful youth: living in Paris as students, as fertile wanderers visiting cafés in all the city's alleys just to feel the enduring effects, of artists of old, that permeate the immutable atmosphere of the most beautiful city in the world.

They smiled and kissed each other's hand as if to say, "Yes, we know you are still here, and our respect for your art and your genius is profound and infinite."

They came out of the café in search of the Seine River and the Île de la Cité. There was a building they needed to admire again: Notre Dame, which had been partially destroyed by a raging fire. Invaluable canvases and paintings were lost forever—who could duplicate them and reestablish their history?

Empty atria, ashy chapels, dozens of agents and volunteers trying to rescue whatever they could—they watched all this, and sorrow clouded their consciousness. Again and again, they admired the immaculate ancient splendor of the famous cathedral; each angle of the domes, each countenance in the paintings, now burnt, played over and over in their memories. Sad were their demeanors as they exited the building.

They stopped for an instant at a balustrade that decorated the Seine's riverbank. There they set their course south, towards the old Spain. This new journey answered a shared desire to be happy people on a happy day in a happy city.

They arrived in Barcelona on a holiday; although, on Barcelona's La Rambla, every day seems like a holiday. The crowd that filled the street oozed, through their attitudes and smiles, the pure joy of being there, under a forgiving sun that shone over all the fortunate passersby.

Suddenly, without the slightest warning, around the corner they made out the ominous silhouette of an enormous white van that was charging towards them at full speed. The crowd did the impossible to make way for the criminal onslaught; clearly the intention was to run over as many pedestrians as possible.

Filled with fear, they saw the van reach a twelve-year-old girl; she disappeared beneath the vehicle and was mangled by its tires. After it crashed into the wall of a clothing store, they watched as the driver pushed the van's door open in haste and tried to escape from the scene of his crime, making way by pushing and punching those who tried to stop him.

Afterwards, despising the impotence of not being able to stop such savagery, Rosa Irena and Pablo Armando sat on a bench outside a cafeteria and saw the immense shadow of death embrace the limp body of the child, as if trying to atone for the infamy of men. Even worse, in that moment, they found out the killer came from a distant land and had been welcomed with open doors by the Spanish and Catalonian governments that gave him the means and opportunity to transform his beggar life with a new job, a home, and enough sustenance. That was how the foreigner repaid the kindness he received—with the shadow of death! It was vengeance without reason, accumulated hatred that had piled up during years and years of schooling in the dark streets of his country! And so was the resentment and ingratitude of that scrap against those who had welcomed him with fondness.

At sunset, they reached the Principality of Asturias. The rocky dam near Pola de Somiedo reflected the sun, and farther away stood the enchanting little town; at its entrance, as a welcome to all travelers, were carved the beautiful traditional barns representative of North Iberia. Some of Pablo Armando's ancestors came from this little town.

They traveled the streets, delighting in the sounds of the clear river that flowed down the mountain, across the town, and trickled in little waterfalls. Then they continued north, towards the sea.

When they reached the fierce coast, they sat on a rocky lookout post and contemplated the Cantabrian Sea. Images of the many battles at sea passed through their minds: tribe against tribe, nation against nation, brother against brother… But a specific battle impacted their spirits: from the north, they saw them come and disembark from narrow wooden ships, their circular shields in hand, the sterns of their ships decorated with fantastic beasts; tall, blond men, shattering with their war axes anyone who stood in their way.

The invasion stopped east of Santander, thanks to the will of the old Basque; they were the mountain sires, the defenders of gods, legends, and old laws— *Jaungoikoa eta lege zaharra.*[1] The legendary, prolific Basque, whose surnames are nurtured by the hay-fields, were a cradle of poor yet intrepid travelers who left behind their own mountains, set their sights on hope from afar, and followed the path of the sun to the immense holy soil of America.

Satisfied with this path, Rosa Irena and Pablo Armando traveled down to La Rioja to contemplate and follow the road of the pilgrimages that headed to beautiful Santiago de Compostela. They stayed long in the city, losing track of time as they mingled with the people who flooded the downtown area, its millennia-old archways and columns made by artists who took the city's secrets to the grave.

All of Santiago was celebrating. It was the gathering point for the Keltic Festival, the biggest in Continental Europe, in honor of that ancient race who had once inhabited those regions of Northern Spain. All around were hefty men in leather shoes and thick wool stockings, decorated with leather laces; men wearing leather

---

[1] God and the old law.

and wool skirts, instead of pants, made from fabrics and designs exclusive to their clans. Hanging from their belts, leather skins containing delicious wine; their shirts, protected by leather or wool vests that also were exclusive to their regions, their people, their mountains; on their heads, wool berets embroidered with their bloodline emblems from a long-past origin.

Every once in a while, groups of virile young men and beautiful young women and children, all dressed and covered in their unique emblems, came down the mountains, towards Santiago, joyfully marching to the beat of their bagpipes. The pride of being Keltic quavered in the air! All at once, Galicians, Asturians, and Santanderinos reaffirmed to the world that their traditions, festivities, and desires were there to stay.

The peace within the walls of Santiago's immense cathedral calmed the unease and profound sadness they'd carried from La Rambla. They had exited intending to enter Portugal through Ourense and Piúca Parish, but the region's calmness changed their mind, and they decided to head to the Tagus River. There, they would join the waves of people in the endless little streets of Toledo, Iberia's first capital.

It was a day like any other when they arrived. The town's history was written on the prehistoric tombs of the first inhabitants and in the turbulence caused by wars. They visited the fortress, which was the backdrop to amazing historic events, both heroic and cruel. Again, the passage of time became tangible before their eyes: the years, the laughter, the tears of those who'd established the name and glory of Toledo in the memory of men; a place of tortures and crownings, the place where the steel that expanded the world was forged. All this was portrayed in paintings inspired by El Greco's genius.

Unable to cry or laugh, Rosa Irena and Pablo Armando shared a hug in mutual understanding.

Seville and Cadiz were just around the corner. America was just a jump away. So they immediately agreed on South Iberia to visit the places that witnessed the valor of man when he is tied to the dream of conquest. In the old Port of Palos, they saw three wooden ships set sail on voyages that would culminate in the amazing news, in a couple of weeks, that there is no drop-off at the edge of the horizon—the world is round; before the sun sets in the west, it shines down on the knowledge of the impossible, an indescribable, pristine new world, nameless still.

From Iberia, they set out for Northern Europe. A little mysterious, a little isolated from the common comings and goings, it was anguished, especially Ukraine. the land of millions of traditions, it had been invaded by the emperor of the perpetual ice region of Siberia. The destruction of their cities and the cruelty of the invaders against Ukraine's populace were testimonies to the permanence of the never-ending desire of man to dominate man, not himself but his neighbor, he whose tongue is foreign, he whose thoughts are foreign, he who looks at foreign horizons. The cruelty that reigned over Ukraine reaffirmed the old proverb *"Homo homini lupus."*[2]

Pablo Armando and Rosa Irene's visit was brutal on their consciousnesses. Scenes of infinite destruction on both sides of the never-ending streets, daily burials for those mowed down by bullets, cannons, missiles, drones, or crushed by invader tanks—it was too horrific to be processed by their minds, even for only an instant. How they wished they could get out of there!

Where did that much hate came from? From a human being with identical cultural roots, traditions, race, and even religion?

A route towards Eastern Europe was necessary to help them understand the reason for the relentless hostility that had already cost half a million dead in two rival countries that were brothers still. The cruelty of the wicked can't be grasped by those consciousnesses that have never thought about hurting a peer. For that very reason, Pablo Armando and Rosa Irene decided to go back to America. But, before

---

[2] Man to man is wolf.

making this jump, they had to go through the lands of Africa and Asia.

Stepping through jungle and desert, they witnessed the unbelievable misery of constant conflicts between people, but also the enormous, tangible hope of the continent where life found itself at the crossroads: continue as apes or dare foresee a different fate. An omen that eventually culminated in the beauty of the poem that shapes the universe and defines it in the final circle of thought; language, will, audacity— Homo sapiens rule the galaxy.

Asia was immense, and it required some time to be covered. As they advanced through the different countries with incomparable cultures, they noticed the leaders, dictators, or those freely elected by their people's will manifested a special kind of fondness for their pets. Most of them had either a horse, a dog, or a cat in their residences. Pets made them and their families happy. The life of the pet seemed to be more valuable than the life of a human being in the eyes of the tyrant dictator or the elected president.

This contrast was obvious in Pablo's and Rosa's minds. How was it possible for a pet to receive more attention and care, in its brief life, than a fellow human being? It seemed irrational to them to believe that the life of a pet could mean more than that of a child or an old person. It was incomprehensible to think that the homes of millions of humans could be summarily destroyed, but the one pet's crate must be protected. And yet, dictators were shown caring for their animals with diligence just to make their subjects think them kind, noble, and caring, thereby negating the notion of their perversity and cruelty.

Our pets are an important part of our lives, and they deserve love and care when they are with us, but it is hypocritical to use them as propaganda to present a false image with the intention of hiding the malice in our treatment of fellow human beings on this beautiful planet.

An immediate concern filled Pablo's and Rosa's minds as they crossed into Asia and were confronted by immense rows of soldiers mobilized by someone's never-ending itch to seize another little piece of land. Who would give the order to kill a brother, to cross the sea and eliminate the lives in neighboring homes? The destruction such longing would cause was frightening and feared. An attack trumpet could sound at any moment, heralding the pending disaster that leads only to death.

Pablo's and Rosa's anguish was unstoppable, so they closed their eyes. Each might've said a prayer for peace, for life.

Chapter II
THE ACCIDENT

Their jump to America was imprecise, for the memories were still fresh in their souls. They relived the moments before the accident, as well as their circumstances before meeting.

Rosa Irene managed a paint factory and was also the translator of files for foreign clients who preferred her company's paints due to the quality of their exclusive formulas. For ten years, she had worked hard in the accounting area, gaining the trust of the factory's owners, to the point that she was promoted to operations manager thanks to her dedication and hard work. She knew, in detail, all the formulas used to prepare each type of paint. Their products were favored by most architects, contractors, and suppliers around the country, and for the last couple of years, by foreign buyers who demanded the best quality.

At thirty-seven, Rosa Irene was in a stable financial position that allowed her to buy a beautiful apartment in a privileged part of town. She chose her friends carefully and only after reflecting on their conduct and personal qualities, their interest in different cultures, and, most of all, their inclinations towards vice, which always ended up destroying relationships and even the spirits of the vicious.

Two possible romantic partners stood out among her small group of friends. One of them was Rogelio Itzcalbalzeta Guillén, the offspring of a settled family whose grandparents had been industrious creators of factories that employed dozens and sometimes even hundreds of workers. Acquired nobly and resolutely, their fortune made them well deserving of the gratitude and respect of those who got to know them or benefited from their kindness and generosity. And yet, Rogelio hadn't inherited the vigor of his ancestors; he barely got through high school and later only earned a degree in business with the help of his ever-present tutors.

His sharp features spoke of his Basque heritage, and his manners were that of the typical spoiled child, a kid accustomed to asking and then immediately receiving. He was a low-level manager in one of the companies established by his father and uncle, his life knew no hiccups, and his interest in Rosa Irene was much more superficial than it appeared. Once, he had been called *"moscardón"*[3] by her because she was tired of his offering her clothing or jewelry she wasn't interested in. Undaunted, Rogelio answered this name-calling with a friendly smile and a promise to be more subtle when approaching her. Despite his promise, Rosa Irene was still not interested in him.

There was another man with an interest in Rosa Irena—José Damián Abreu, a nervous man who had established a little business that sold windows and aluminum frames. Thanks to increased demands for the construction of houses and buildings in the growing, turbulent city, he had prospered enough to partner with a construction company with offices in two of the major cities of the country.

He met Rosa Irene a couple of years before the accident, when some of the representatives of the construction company met with her to sign a contract for the paint for one of their buildings. Abreu was invited to the meeting and then, later, to a dinner to celebrate the contract. After this encounter, their friendship grew and grew until it was a formal romantic relationship. On his part, Rogelio showed no signs of jealousy

---

[3] Literally translated, it is a blowfly, but colloquially this term is used to refer to an insistent man, an unrelenting suitor whose unwanted flirting is annoying.

and instead congratulated them on their relationship and wished them well in the future.

Things between Rosa Irene and Abreu were good until the day the construction company announced they wanted to open a window and aluminum-frame factory in another city where they already had a branch. This way, they would save on third-party services while still providing contractors and future owners of the buildings quality products manufactured in their own city. The company asked Abreu to move to that city to formally set up the factory.

When Rosa Irene heard about it, she showed none of the concern the news caused her. Abreu's estimated absence of six months was extended to a year, and though they promised to be in constant contact, over time, their communication became less and less frequent, until it finally ended when Abreu let Rosa know that he had met a woman in the other city, their attraction was mutual, she came from an excellent family, she had had the privilege of a meticulous, one-of-a-kind education, they both loved sports, etc., etc., etc. And so, Rosa Irene's relationship ended.

Though in different years, Pablo Armando and Rosa Irene had studied in Paris. Rosa Irene was the only child of a prosperous Spanish immigrant born in the outskirts of Zaragoza. He started by selling little machines that analyzed samples of blood; he sacrificed food and clothing in the name of his savings. Selling such machines, he reached a certain level of prestige, and with the daring that characterized him, he established a small branch in the second-most important city in the country. In just a few years of hard, intelligent, honest work, he secured the exclusive franchise to import the analyzers, which eventually became the standard for laboratories, hospitals, clinics, and certain doctors' offices. His fortune permitted him to send his daughter, Rosa Irene, to study abroad at one of those famous summer courses offered by Parisian universities.

Young Rosa Irene filled her time by wandering the immense city, rather than studying useless courses like French culinary art, the untold story of the French Revolution, the evolution of abstract art in France and Europe, and others that similarly bored even the teachers. Yes, in those three consecutive years that her father invested his money in his adored daughter's education, she learned a bit, mostly French, but the main attraction for her was being away from her father's vigilant eyes.

It eventually ended when Don Alejandro, Rosa Irene's father, suffered an esophageal rupture, the consequence of a peptic ulcer and years and years of anxiety and perpetual pressures to prosper and "make it." Possessing the noble, yet cold, immutable character that was forged by formative years lived with political perils that forced him to leave his country and search for refugee in distant lands, he was only obeying an instinct to thrive when he ignored the first symptom: a deep pain in his chest that he tried to calm by over-dosing on antacids.

His passing was disastrous for Rosa Irene. She suffered a depression so severe that it had to ultimately be controlled with accurate doses of medication that helped her regain the necessary optimism to defeat the sadness and fill the enormous void the parting of a loved one leaves. She was able to finish her undergraduate degree in marketing, receive a master's in international finance, and take specialized courses on import/export regulations offered by the great banking institutions of America and Europe. This curriculum, when added to her natural intelligence and stubbornness, made it easier for her to manage the important paint factory for which she was now its chairman.

* * *

On the other hand, Pablo Armando led a life of ups and downs in his career and interpersonal relationships. He graduated as an architect from the national university and obtained a master's degree in design and material resistance. He directed the design area in an architectural firm with countless projects in the city. Pablo adjusted, reluctantly, to the demands of the owners of the firm, who liked futuristic silhouettes for their building designs, despite Pablo Armando's insistence, as frequently as possible, on classic, more traditional shapes, for, according to him, "the classics never go out of style."

This attitude had already caused quite a few difficulties with the directors of the company. Even though they truly appreciated Pablo for adding a unique and acclaimed design style to the firm, they couldn't allow him to impose his own wishes over those of the buildings' owners who had hired the firm. Eventually, they struck a happy medium: Pablo's classic designs would be used on small construction jobs, while the larger buildings would maintain their modernist forms. This appeased Pablo Armando, who was already contemplating quitting and searching for a firm more in line with his vision as an architect.

His private life also had hiccups. His girlfriend, Leticia Navarro de Cáceres, was a privileged young woman who was dazzled by the sterile monologues of the social circle she and her friends frequented. She and her friends had the same outlook on life: have a good time, create chaos when opportune, and be current in all gossip.

"Why, yes, *chulis*,[4] Jorge Montenegro, the new heartthrob of the telenovela *El Gallinazo de Cujitalpa*, has been seen with Mariquita de la Vega in a quite

---

[4] Cutie.

compromising position. This might be the reason behind her divorce from the composer Avendaño Henriquez."

Leticia's circle of friends consisted of some women with degrees, others certified in not-so-meaningful-to-daily-life areas like cosmetology, and still others taking advanced courses on rejuvenating cremes, which were offered by the French Institute of Hair and Makeup for Actresses. Generally, the ideas of this group of friends were as strange as they were funny.

The psychologist of the group claimed that going to heaven meant you could "create chaos with the chosen ones in paradise forever and ever and ever." Similarly, the "herbatologist" swore by the extraordinary healing effects of the renowned capulin oil; it supposedly cured everything from the most insignificant of colds to the most terminal of cancers. And, of course, anything in the middle, such as correcting bunions and making the deaf-mute speak.

This group also included certain boastful doctors who were even more phony than they seemed. Some of them, after finishing their studies, went away to take a course for two or three weeks, a little symposium about hematological illnesses or a specific type of cancer, somewhere in Texas. They came back declaring they were oncologists or hematologists, and yet they could not prove they had correctly finished the six required years of study in any subspecialty. Others claimed to be researchers and even published articles about the untested benefits of the scorpion's-tail plant, saying it was capable of healing prostate cancer and increasing libido. Of course, it was sold exclusively by the article's author.

Their audacity was such that if an ill patient arrived at their consult seeking treatment, they would make up illnesses just to sell them expensive medicines that were about to expire. And so the real illness went untreated. This sometimes caused fatalities or irreparable damage to the patients.

Their mercenariness was a disgrace and a blight on the noble profession of medicine, and yet Leticia was happy to frequent the circle, within which conversations always revolved around the trivial. Their recreational days almost always ended in states of euphoria caused by micro doses of this or that drug. But, little by little, the micro doses stopped being so micro, and as the need to acquire drugs increased, so did the financial pressures on Leticia's life to fund her "recreation." Her addiction grew and demanded higher doses to reach those states of euphoria that removed her from reality and robbed her of direction and the impulse to help others, to be of importance to those she saw pass through the vortex that her life had become.

To face this situation, Pablo Armando waited for the right moment to talk to her about what had been going on, which was preventing their relationship from developing in the best way possible.

Leticia was adamant in her response: she denied using any narcotics and accused Pablo of failing to give her enough attention. So he ended the conversation by inviting her on a date, which she rejected. He left, alone, to listen to a piano concert at a convent he had loved since he started his studies.

* * *

Weeks before the concert, in an abstract-art exhibit in Palacio de Bellas Artes, where they were showing pieces by Van Gogh, Pablo noted something about one of the paintings, and he shared it with one of the young women who was also admiring the painting of the eccentric Van Gogh. The comment preceded a quite cordial invitation by Pablo to have something to eat in the little cafeteria of the palace, which is on the first floor of Bellas Artes and the delight of exhibit or function attendees.

Their conversation was cordial and animated, for they found they had both studied in Paris. Pablo noted that one of his courses had been about the evolution of architecture in France, and the young woman mentioned she took one on the evolution of the culinary arts. They remembered the jokes Parisians make about the metro and the disgust they felt upon finding out that some restaurants offered horse meat on their menus. With no anticipation of a future encounter, they departed sometime later and went their separate ways.

And so, as mentioned, Pablo arrived to the concert by himself. Before it started, he recognized *her*, Rosa Irene, the woman he had met at the Van Gogh exhibit. He approached her, and she politely greeted and invited him to sit beside her, for her partner, Abreu, was out of town.

Silently, they enjoyed the magnificent concert, and as it ended, this time they did agree to meet again for dinner at a restaurant located in one of the buildings designed by Pablo Armando. By then, Abreu had already notified Rosa Irene about his interest in somebody else. Similarly, Pablo Armando was starting to distance himself from Leticia, as he had already concluded that he wasn't capable of changing the direction she had chosen.

Dinner was the beginning of a friendship that ended in a romantic relationship. Pablo Armando moved to an apartment farther from the one he shared with Leticia and closer to Rosa Irene. As time went on, they decided to share their lives and rented an apartment together. Friendship and empathy were the basis of their mutual way of understanding and resolving daily problems. There was an ever-predictable question: "Can I help?"

One time, as they chatted in their living room and sunlight came in through the window, Rosa Irena noticed the way it reflected in Pablo's eyes. It was unusual. His eyes, really, were nothing particularly special, yet Rosa Irene took that chance to say, with tenderness in every word, "Well, Pablo, you have the eyes of a cat!"

Pablo's answer to such a strange observation was a kind smile and an invitation to have pistachio ice cream at the corner *nevería*.[5]

Their lives went on as usual, and a certain rainy July weekend, they decided to visit a near town that had the privilege of being connected to the capital by a highway. They gladly packed and got in the car with no bad omen in sight.

It all went as planned. The air between them was infused with a unity of desires, realities, and promises. They had never had banal fights; they were meant for each other.

As they went around a curve in the road, suddenly they saw construction trailers and other vehicles working on a piece of the highway. There was loose gravel on the road, their multilane highway had turned

---

[5] A shop where nieves are sold. Nieves are a Mexican type of ice cream, typically less creamy and fresher than other ice cream, as it is water based and often made with fresh fruit.

into only one lane for the cars going down the hill, and there were no warning signs to lower their speed before reaching the curve. Instead, these warnings were placed after the curve, a few meters before the first construction vehicle.

Pablo Armando hit the brakes abruptly on the wet, slippery surface of the highway; to make matters worse, the gravel from the trailers, dispersed by wind and other vehicles, covered the highway and gave the tires no traction with which to stop. The tires slid, and Pablo Armando lost control of the car, which rolled and flew over the median, into the opposite lanes of the highway, crashing against the metal guardrail that protected cars from driving into a fifteen-meter-deep ditch.

An even greater tragedy was averted by the guardrail and the fact that no other cars were on the highway at the time of the accident going up toward the capital. As the car rolled, Pablo Armando saw the pavement approaching his face at an indescribable speed. He closed his eyes and held on to the steering wheel as hard as he could. He felt Rosa Irene's head impact his, and instantly he lost consciousness and all sense of the "after."

Days later, he woke up in a hospital bed, in the city, and realized he had suffered no serious damage to any vital organs. Rosa Irene, who was standing beside the bed, cheering him on, didn't seem bruised or seriously injured either. They listened to the doctors' conversations; they were sure neither one of them needed further medical attention, so their families could take them back home to the capital.

When they arrived at their apartment, they felt a strange sensation that the apartment was a bit different from the one they had rented and lived in for countless happy hours Spaces seemed bigger, and they found it easier to move from one place to another. These sensations, they concluded, were explained by the possibility that their long stay in the hospital had made them lose a lot of weight. They went through their belongings and found everything was as they had left it before the accident.

As they left the apartment and walked down the street, their consciousnesses transported them to experiences prior to the accident, which signaled to their minds that they now had the ability to decide which exact moment they wanted to explore, even if it meant going back to a timeline different from the one that contained the very instant they were currently inhabiting. And this filled them with joy, for, together, they now could walk the routes they had always wanted to explore yet couldn't, as they had opted at the time to make the decisions that led them to other paths. They also noticed that their desire to walk this or that route coincided. This as well filled them with joy, but only after they recovered from the surprise and awe at what was unraveling before them.

They had to leave for later the full exploration of this new state of consciousness, for at the moment, their presence was needed at a reunion their friends and family had organized at some place to celebrate their lives and the opportunity to again be together, and to wish them luck on the trip they were planning to take together as a well-deserved gift after the terrible accident they'd survived.

The stories of longing and shared moments moved the attendees of the reunion to laughter and tears. Some of them spoke; others just listened. They mentioned how noble Rosa and Pablo were and all the promises that wouldn't be forgotten until they would meet again.

Rosa and Pablo noted that, when the attendees greeted each other, their demeanors and actions were effusive. This contrasted with the seriousness in the attendees' faces when they approached Rosa and Pablo.

So Rosa and Pablo were patient. They listened to their friends' jokes with a smile on their faces and remembered their shenanigans as children and youths, the memories of which were being shared by their friends: Pablo's little quarrels with his school peers, Rosa's absurd hairstyle in high school, etc. In the end, the attendees wished Rosa and Pablo the best of luck and said prayers for their next journey.

Rosa Irene and Pablo Armando remained silent throughout the proceedings, and when it was over, filled with an immaculate inner peace that seemed to manifest the force of their joint desires, they exited the room. This force poured over them, flooding their souls, as had the love and friendship of those who had shared their paths in life.

Chapter III

MOUNDS OF LIGHT AND WALLS OF DARKNESS

I n the street, Rosa Irene and Pablo Armando contemplated the immense city, ever growing, exceeding its own limits and extending into other regions. Their apartment now seemed like a minuscule point of reference, and yet it was there that they agreed on exploring every one of the possible places on their journey.

They had a supreme ability, a fate reserved only for the chosen ones by destiny: the immutable force that decrees and rules what's to happen with each mortal. However, our will is an essential part of this force: whether we know it or not, we choose what happens to us. The future is, then, the result of that election. An unavoidable conclusion; however, in "the after," beyond that conclusion, the power of consciousness exceeds the limits of destiny, allowing us to discover where a decision could have ended, or the next decision, or the next, or the next, ad infinitum...

Rosa Irene's and Pablo Armando's first impulse was to travel to countries ruled by tyrant dictators, several of whom still persist in the Americas. There was a common denominator among all of them: the deceiving of the population to achieve power and then the consolidation of such power via the brutality of weapons. Once power was gained, there was no need to keep any of the promises given to the unsuspecting ones who would eventually face the severe consequences for having believed the tyrants' lies.

As they passed through those countries, they saw impotence reflected on some of the faces of the inhabitants, regret on others, resignation on still others. Sardonicism on the faces of dictators and their accomplices and reigning mediocrity in attitudes towards work, towards the future, on the majority of the faces of the deceived who now had to find a way to survive with only the bare minimum.

The conformism of the oppressed by the dictatorships in feigning happiness when notified that they were perfect candidates to receive the *sueldito*,[6] or government handouts. "There, there, we now have

---

[6] Literally, little salary.

the coupon for an extra pound of sugar, half a dozen eggs, ten slices of bread, two toilet-paper rolls... Now we can invite over the neighborhood official! We can even offer, 'Sir, would you care for a cup of coffee? Sugar or no sugar? What about a piece of bread to go with it?' Because, woman, we must get on the official's good side. Who knows if in the next meeting, when he announces the neighbors' merit positions, he could gift us with a coupon for *four* extra toilet-paper rolls. Then we wouldn't need to use the pages of the official newspaper they distribute every two weeks so we find out about all the amazing work our leader is doing with such effort for the benefit of all his people!

"Though, let me tell you, I once was in the official's house, just to let him know that one of the neighbors had been talking crap about our leader, and I noticed that, in his living room, he only had the covers of the newspaper, no interior pages! I said nothing, obviously, and I believe he thanked me for it, for in the next neighborhood meeting, he allowed me to buy a pair of socks.

"Anyway, with four toilet-paper rolls, we wouldn't have to use the leaves from our mango tree. This year, it didn't give us as much fruit, but I've told you, woman, mango trees are like that: the fewer leaves they have, the fewer mangoes they give!"

This was the way life went for those subjugated and resigned to the dictatorships' brutality! But if some fortunate person won an Olympic medal, he was deserving of a "bigger" little house, perhaps one with a garden to plant an orange or a lemon tree.

What about the tyrant's grandchildren? Why, they have their own bodyguards and a mansion in Paris!

The dictator and his pack rob their people of all their liberties while they amass all their own rights. There's no mercy in a dictator. But there's also no peace for the wicked; they'll always walk with their backs to the wall, always be surrounded by their *hampa*[7] bodyguards, always be reluctant to close their eyes because they are afraid they'll never open them again—that's our America, full of traitors, thieves, and murderers, full of corruption and sycophancy. Governed by a fallacy that has studied the ignorance of its people, so they are shamelessly offered little jars of distilled water that they claim is filled with medicine; full of stupidity, insignificance, and adoration of the vain and superfluous; full of promises never kept; a dead-end path bordered by the praying lips of our mothers, our grandmothers…

There's no mercy in dictators.

---

[7] Criminals organized in gangs, each with specific rules of conduct.

In the citizens oppressed by their power, a soft, pale light of hope can only be guessed at. Our people's 200 years of history and participation in freedom are not much when compared to this world's millions of turns. Maybe, someday, we will be given the impulse to correct our direction. Maybe that's why we should keep waiting.

In their meandering through the immensity of the continent, Rosa and Pablo began feeling an aura of eternity when, suddenly, their path was met with mounds of light for which they didn't know the meaning yet. This wonderful phenomenon happened at equal intervals during their journey. They admired it; it infused them with a sense of unmatched well-being. *What could be the origin of those mounds?* they each wondered.

In front of the one that seemed to be the biggest yet, they stopped for an unplanned, brief moment and hugged each other just to see if they could make the sensation that radiated from it even grander. It surrounded them with a halo of joy. And so they were reassured that not everything was lost in our dear America, that there was a signal higher than the sludge formed by the tyrants, one just the same as the other, indistinguishable, who had sunk millions of our people. Yes, the force this mound emitted hit Rosa's and Pablo's consciousness with a flow of ripe words, unpronounced yet pronounceable.

What's that feeling that foresees a good harvest in the ideas man dreams of when facing his own misery? Maybe they'd find out farther ahead.

They contemplated the unheard-of poverty and suffering that stands out in the immensity of Africa, Asia, and South America, products of the arrogance of the few. This made their spirits tremble; injustice always makes the spirit tremble. As they saw, they bowed their heads; discouraged, they went on their way, trying to reach their native country.

Back in it, they decided to cross the northern border into the United States. The immensity of its land brought them the feeling that this country was made to survive for eternity. Yet, as they progressed through the streets, the cities, they got the vague sensation of something ominous.

Something was happening, something was about to happen in that far-off, beautiful country that planted its flag on a distant surface, beyond the reach of envy and even beyond the force of gravity. Something was happening, and it was tangible in the nation's soul.

They watched the most unbelievable things: children gunning down other children at schools; mobs of youngsters insulting other youngsters and even preventing them from expressing themselves; hordes of masked people breaking into shops and houses, smashing glass and filling their pockets and large plastic bags with jewels and clothing. And in their demeanors, a sense of impunity was clear. It was evident that they had colluded with judges and prosecutors.

Something was happening in that beautiful country, something soft and profound, something that mangled the teachings of their ancestors, their old principles: freedom for all, equality before the Supreme Creator and before all men. Something was happening, and it nagged at the consciousness, the soul of the land. The hunt of the many to reach the very well-known ends could be perceived; they wanted to oppress with false flags, false promises, so as to wield the threat of jail so no one would dare oppose them.

That funeral march must be stopped. They had to return to what was sacred, the origin of the youngest and most powerful nucleus of earth.

Something was happening in that beautiful country, something soft and profound. It seemed that the superfluous or the mediocre had triumphed! And so did the love for laziness and inconsequential futility. This love was filtering down, and it was causing a certain drowsiness in the audacity of the men who had conquered space and science.

Yet, as ever, endangered societies wait for a revolution that will shake their minds, stop them from falling into a bottomless pit. Waking up the wise, the poets, all good men, was imperative. The direction had to be corrected, and if it came down to it and the soul of the country was in mortal peril, the loyal general must be called. He must throw away the useless ballet shoes and replace them with combat boots.

Something was happening in that beautiful country. Something soft and yet profound that filled Rosa Irene and Pablo Armando's consciousness with something ominous.

Even though Canada was just around the corner, Rosa Irene wanted to go back to Europe. Old Europe, birthplace of the culture that dictates our lives, of world-transforming wisdom; the scenario of wars, persecutions, a million dead. There stood the old nations.

Romania, the Latin island in the center of a sea of tumultuous Slavs; beautiful Croatia, ever the defender of Christianity; old Bulgaria, its prehistory yet untold; rigid Polonia, victor over impertinent slavery and now the tip of the spear against the East. Polonia's glory has been long-winded, and their strength of spirit is untamable. The Northern Lands, now the richest in the world, thanks to their vigor and integrity of character; ancient Serbia, heart of the Etruscans, starting point of the lineage that later was established in the skirts of the Latio, only to then expand through tongue and sword till they surrounded the Mediterranean and formed the greatest empire of the ancient world, Rome, whose influence is the mold that still shapes our culture, our lives. Rome is the empire that drove and defined the start and end of the ages.

Beautiful Europe, beautiful Europe, your history knows of war and misfortune, and yet many times you were favored with the fortunes of intellectuality, that which is made of the hard, prolific work of a few and still reaches the homes of the many.

Germany, Germany, dear Germany.

Mother Russia, Mother Russia, what have you been doing? The drumming of your cannons pointing to the sky, to the angels, can still be heard.

Europe, make no excuses. Beautiful Europe, we know about your ways, the old wandering of your centuries. You've never enjoyed peace for more than a second, a full generation, not even for the span of a motion made against the death of still more children. Oh, Europe!

Beautiful Europe, where the offshoot who expanded the world was created, the one who invented the riddle of science, the one who embraced a lineage of wisemen, those who depicted soul, anguish, fierceness, pride, impotence in the face of death. The necessity to explain that which hasn't been explained, to silence death's roar with music, the one where only Bach's and Beethoven's notes are heard.

They reached Germany with a better understanding of eternity, which is common in the prevalent atmosphere of Europe. Before going any farther, they shared a slow, silent embrace, as they had before traveling through America. Throughout their steps, they again were met with small and large mounds of light, and finally they deciphered their meaning. They were the announcements of the geniuses and prophets who changed the sense and sensibility of men. The whole universe stopped before such apparitions; it seemed to delight in the knowledge that something invincible had been born.

Miracles can't be defeated. That's why peace was prevalent when the mounds first appeared. Rosa Irene and Pablo Armando witnessed that peace, and they admired it as often as it crossed their path. Yet their faces reflected anguish as they heard the groans and moans of war. How long had that specter followed them? It was hard to tell, even though they insisted on looking back. The beginning of life, the beginning of language, the beginning of law, the beginning of hate. It was hard for them to watch as art faded, as did its conquests; to watch as laughter was robbed from a child by a cruel hand; to watch the course of a missile launched far from what it would destroy, a tyrant's command.

For them, it was imperative to head south towards Italy.

Everlasting Italy, creator of multiple cultures, races, nations, dreams, and legends. They smiled at each other when they saw the vigorous countenance of some people contrast with the supreme calmness of others, those whose fibers were made of the stern, firm, proud, and invincible past of the Romans who built cities and paved roads that always led back to Rome. History, law, and justice sprouted there, and they remain in the teachings of the wise, the ones who are aware of their past and their future. From there sprouted a language that would change all the ideas that now inhabit our lives, our reason for being.

In the Roman Forum, they saw a parade of victims and perpetrators, cowards and heroes, faithful and pagan; those who lived only for the pleasure of spilled blood and those martyrs whose lives were ended for the pride of a Caesar; those who took their places among the saints. They saw the streets of Florence, its museums; Michelangelo's *David* and his frescoes in the Sistine Chapel; Hercules's and Artemisia's temples; Trajan's Column; and his victory over the ancient Serbians: the irony of knowing that his origin, his lineage came from the Etruscans. And then, the solemn immensity of Saint Peter's Cathedral. It all seemed meant to be eternal, to remain for perpetuity in Italy. Even in the simplicity of a football match, everything in Italy is eternal. Our Italy.

In Italy, Rosa Irene and Pablo Armando went through the changes that their consciousness was begging them to make. Everything started to feel different after the accident. Yes, they understood that their natural origin was in America; that was their home. Their journeys filled them with enthusiasm for having found a reason for their destiny.

They were alone in some place they understood was named Italy, and the journey to get there and their stay had only taken a split second of the time they still had. These new feelings had nothing to do with the fact that they had no appetite, not even for the delicacies they passed. Actually, they came to realize that they hadn't had anything to eat since the accident, and yet this didn't spark their curiosity too much, for they had always been frugal in their eating habits.

And so they became aware of the extraordinary question: Was it possible that the accident transported them to an exclusive shared dimension? There was no one like them around, and yet they felt no loneliness. "We were born for each other," they had repeated several times before the accident.

Another new thing they perceived as they progressed through Europe was that the echo of a step or the murmur of a voice is never lost; it leaves a stamp that remains forever in a corner of time. How else would it be possible for them to listen to Napoleon's words to his soldiers as their steps took them through the meadows of France and the plains of Belgium, straight to the last battle of the French emperor against the military genius of the English? How else could they listen to the soft splashing of the water as Pontius Pilate washed his hands on Christ's last day on earth? How else could they hear Isaiah's sentence defining peace between men: "A bruised reed he will not break, and a smoldering wick he will not snuff out"? Or his incredible vision for what the future held when he wrote, 160 years before the Persian emperor of the ancient world was born: " Cyrus, Cyrus, I'm calling you by name so you know who I am!"?

As Rosa Irene and Pablo Armando had more experiences, they deduced that consciousness, the prime faculty of man, is carried within him forever; no matter the transitions he suffers, his perception remains, reminding him of what he used to be. This is the requirement to remain, the permanent seal that constitutes our identity and separates us from others. Even beyond sensibility, consciousness gives us a name, our pride.

There, in that moment of consciousness, Rosa Irene and Pablo Armando identified each other. They seemed to be one and the same, though the littlest differences reminded each one who they were; one was Rosa Irene and the other Pablo Armando. Between them remained a space so, so, so small, almost imperceptible, though their consciousnesses knew and wouldn't forget until the end of times.

What if time had stood still? The trust they were filled with caused them such tenderness for each other, and they immediately understood that not having hurt anyone awarded them transcendence towards truth, no explanation needed.

They had been good. And the reward was ever the same; consciousness promised them they must wait for the reward with no fear. Yet in this never-ending state, it couldn't be assumed that the direction would always tend towards forever. No, never. They were experiencing the shoves of their consciousnesses towards walkable places, and they were filled with satisfaction for having been able to walk hand in hand until they came back to their starting point. That is what's strange and impossible to change: the never-ending return to the starting point, where you have to decide what's next...*ad infinitum*.

That's what eternity is, they realized: the choice to follow each road to its end even though, before, they had selected other paths. Eternity is a place to resolve all doubts as one experiences all possibilities. So if life allows us to decide on this or that specific road, eternity allows us to explore every one of the ones not taken. How many seconds make up our lives? How many seconds make up eternity? Eternity offers only a forward destination that can never be reached. No other option.

The opportunity given depends on the feeling and the will projected in life. Rosa Irena and Pablo Armando had filled their laps with good sentiments, good will, and they remained together because of it. Still holding each other's hand, in each other's arms, an undeniable embrace. With them was the hope that held all treasures to pay for the box in the theater: all the chapters, minutes, seconds of life passing by. Now they had to continue, to walk back each of the seconds that had led them there, towards the end. No arguments left, no more options.

They laughed at the thought that the famous mandate by Antonio Machado, "*Caminante no hay camino, sino estelas en la mar,*"[8] could easily be changed to "*Caminante sí hay camino, como estelas en la mar.*"[9]

Eventually, Rosa Irene and Pablo Armando agreed on exploring every possible path they had ignored in life and had so regretted, wondering if one of them would have taken them to a happy ending.

---

[8] Wayfarer, there is no path, only wake trails in the sea.
[9] Wayfarer, there is a path, like wake trails in the sea.

Irene explored one of those ways, the one that started in Palacio de Bellas Artes, in the company of Damián Abreu, who had suggested they go home before seeing all the paintings in the Van Gogh exhibit. She refused and, this upset Damián, who decided to go home alone, which resulted in the official goodbye to spending their lives together, as moments after Damián left, Pablo Armando arrived, made his comments about Van Gogh's art, which caused Irene to respond with her own comments, sparking their friendship.

She also explored another one. She didn't stay in Palacio de Bellas Artes; she went home with Damián, and after that, the faults in his character were clear to her until a dark, impossible-to-pass-through wall met her, making her go back to the starting point.

Irene explored many other paths; some really seemed to end in happiness or at least a lasting satisfaction, but they all ended similarly: no kids, disenchantments, solitude, and that thick wall that stopped her from going yet another step other than back to the starting point.

Pablo Armando also walked other paths. First, the one that started as he studied *Starry Night*, seconds before making a comment to Irene. A mere instant before, he was experiencing anguish: job problems, relationship problems. "I have no interest in those kinds of paintings" was Leticia's dry response.

And so Pablo tried that path too. After missing the exhibit, his life was filled with uneasiness beside a selfish wife with explosive outbursts of emotions, such as crying for no reason, screaming for no reason... Her dependence on drugs robbed her of her personality and pushed her towards an immense desert from which she never emerged. Pablo Armando reached the end of that path with a torn soul. Before him stood a dark wall, impenetrable, from which point he was unable to look further until he was back at the starting point.

Close to each other, they realized their journey together was the best way possible, for the inextricable threads of love tied them together.

Farther ahead, they came upon an immense, endless valley. There they encountered a sign as old as the world itself, written in all languages, understandable to any and all: SO TIME STOOD STILL.

Epilogue

AND SO SPOKE
THE POET

L isten:

It was all conceived by voice. It was all born out of a scream that turned to foam.

Thought elevates in the arpeggio of genius.

Look at it arrive, little suitcase in hand, searching for refuge through alleys and dark garrets.

It has hidden in the big cities, and neither its beginning nor its end is circled by the whirlwind of numbers.

Behind or beyond what's impossible, it deciphers the words that define beauty.

The stamp of its infancy.

The parchment keeps it from the mundane, comprehensible language.

Why do you speak of such "important" matters if no one, or almost no one, sweetens misery or shushes a tumultuous soul with birds' subtle language?

It finds comfort in the sublime notes of music. It finds its hiding place and with the tips of its fingers traces unknown paths to remind us of our value, our nobility.

Yet it always stays behind to signal paths discovered in the fertility of dreams. Its dream, the will that pushes us to leave what's notable for what has never been, and yet for it, it will be. For it, it will be palpable and reformable for whoever dares reform it.

A disruption in the soul, unique, sublime, made for a never-written story, fitted to a hymn not yet heard.

A composition of phrases that defines life today and life tomorrow...

Who will dare measure up against such force?

Who dares submerge it in a prison?

Who here has the audacity to imitate it, to steal a word from it, a note, a shard of its sphere?

I apologize if you don't understand.

I apologize for any confusion.

The jump to what's infinite can carry no shadows to stop it. It's better to remain. Routine is good; it perceives none of the pain caused by the creation of the world, caused by a future so near it engulfs us all, even those who doubted, even those who shushed the subtle language of birds.

About Rosa Irene and Pablo Armando, there remains only the knowledge that they were in the place where the privilege of having been was marked. Their encounter was fair and necessary to outpace the injustices of destiny. Of their embrace, we can only guess at happiness, as our only possession is knowing we will be different even if we do not change.

There are no endings left. That, we have established.

From here, Rosa Irene's and Pablo Armando's backs can still be gazed at as they slowly walk away.

Go with them.

I dare you.

AUTHOR'S NOTE

S o *Time Stood Still* is the third book in the trilogy, *On the Right to Peace*. The poetic principle for it is established here: "It was all conceived by voice. It was all born out of a scream that turned to foam," and in the possible existence of a blue space where almost anything is possible, including our shared dream: a lasting peace. This can be already guessed at in the first book of the trilogy, *Book of Omens*, in which the perception of the light as a symbol of hope for a world that suffers injustices and the horrors of war. This hope sprang even before life itself.

The genius of man, the scientists in the second book, *Spring of Light*, points at the knowledge of the present that leads to the origin of the light that holds an immense treasure within, ready to be distributed among all human beings, so to bring them riches and comfort, avoiding envy and conflict, as they survive war and loss.

What's offered in this third book is a way to obtain a lasting peace between the peoples. Here, the paths of an ideal couple who never hurt anyone are narrated as we refer to the potential of the spirit of man (men and women) to get to an ideal place, that poetic blue, where the wishes of the people are granted: a lasting peace in which time stands still.

The trilogy about peace (to which we all have the right):

1. *Book of Omens*
2. *Spring of Light*
3. *So Time Stood Still*

To enjoy the taste of the idea, the offer, and get to the happy ending, this order must be followed.

"Albarda, escudo y lanza. Ese es el orden, Sancho".

Renato Bettio

ABOUT THE AUTHOR

Roberto Arévalo Araujo MD, FACP, (Renato Bettio) was born in El Salvador. After high school, he traveled to Mexico to continue his studies and was certified as a physician and surgeon by the Facultad de Medicina of the UNAM in Mexico City, 1970. He then interned in the Oakwood Hospital (Dearborn, Michigan), followed by two years in internal medicine at the University of Medicine and Dentistry of New Jersey (UMDNJ). In the three following years, he specialized in hematology and oncology at UMDNJ. He is board-certified in internal medicine, hematology, and medical oncology.

He is a fellow of the American College of Physicians and the founder of the Cancer and Hematology Center in Pasco and Pinellas Counties, Florida, where they offer radiotherapy, chemotherapy, and immuno-therapy. He is also a founder of the Medical Mission of Mercy / Medical Mission International, whose objective is to freely offer surgical and ophthalmological help to homeless people in El Salvador. In 2002, the mission was nominated for a Nobel Peace Prize.

Now, he brings to you, dear reader, a piece of the inspiration his soul embraces. He writes stories about impunity and misery that affect his Central American fellow countrymen. Yet he also ascribes himself to the tangible faith of those affected. In them, in spite of their suffering, the longing for life doesn't go out; they have a philosophy that keeps them thinking that it's better to be.

Book of Omens
ISBN Paperback: 978-1-63765-625-9
Paperback Price: $14.95
Page Count: 126

This book follows the journey of a dream that begins in youth, explored in Longings and A Poetry of Absence. As despair looms under felonious leaders, hope rises in The Light, where the long-ignored finally triumph. Spring of Light dissects a world-changing discovery meant for the noble and generous, serving only peace. Las Comadres brings humor and wisdom through the everyday lives of intuitive, unchanging women. And for those who still dream, Adventures in Poetry offers a final gift of verse.

Spring of Light
ISBN Paperback: 978-1-63765-732-4
Paperback Price: $18.95
Page Count: 248

www.ingramcontent.com/pod-product-compliance
Lightning Source LLC
Chambersburg PA
CBHW071143250626
47159CB00006B/2282